BEASTLY Basil

Tessa Krailing

Illustrated by
Mike Phillips

OXFORD
UNIVERSITY PRESS

OXFORD
UNIVERSITY PRESS

Great Clarendon Street, Oxford OX2 6DP

Oxford University Press is a department of the University of Oxford.
It furthers the University's objective of excellence in research, scholarship,
and education by publishing worldwide in

Oxford   New York

Auckland   Cape Town   Dar es Salaam   Hong Kong   Karachi
Kuala Lumpur   Madrid   Melbourne   Mexico City   Nairobi
New Delhi   Shanghai   Taipei   Toronto

With offices in

Argentina   Austria   Brazil   Chile   Czech Republic   France   Greece
Guatemala   Hungary   Italy   Japan   Poland   Portugal   Singapore
South Korea   Switzerland   Thailand   Turkey   Ukraine   Vietnam

Oxford is a registered trade mark of Oxford University Press
in the UK and in certain other countries

British Library Cataloguing in Publication Data

Data available

ISBN 978-0-19-915190-5

5 7 9 10 8 6

Mixed Pack (1 of 6 different titles): ISBN 978-0-19-915184-4
Class Pack (6 copies of 6 titles): ISBN 978-0-19-915183-7

Printed in China by Imago

Contents

Chapter 1

A Shameful Secret

Everyone agreed that Beastly Basil
was a very handsome little monster.
His teeth were yellow and pointed
like a wolf's. His eyes gleamed and he
had purple spots all over his skin.

All the other little monsters
admired him.

"He's so good-looking!" sighed
Sickening Susan.

"Like a movie star," sighed
Boastful Bertha.

"I wish I looked like he does," said
Disgusting Denzil, who was Basil's
best friend.

But in spite of all this, Beastly Basil was not happy.

In fact, Basil was worried ... because he had a shameful secret – a secret only known to himself and his parents. And now he was scared the other little monsters would find out ...

The trouble started on Monday morning at school.

"I have some exciting news," said Dr Grim, the head teacher. "This year, we're having a Summer Camp at Whispering Woods. Please put up your hands if you would like to come."

With a shriek of delight, all the little monsters put up their hands. That is, all except Beastly Basil.

"What's the matter, Baz?" asked Disgusting Denzil. "Don't you want to come?"

"I'm not sure," said Basil, cautiously. "It depends on the date."

Disgusting Denzil waved his arm at Dr Grim. "Please, Sir, when do we go to Camp?"

"From the 25th to the 31st July," said Dr Grim.

Basil frowned. He did some quick sums on his fingers. Then he shook his head. "I can't come," he said.

"Why not?" asked Sickening Susan.

"Because I can't, that's why!" snapped Basil.

The others stared at him. It wasn't like Basil to be snappy. He was usually so polite and good-tempered.

"But you *must*," said Disgusting Denzil. "It won't be the same without you."

"Just think what you'll be missing," said Boastful Bertha. "Sleeping in a tent under the stars ..."

"Cooking over an open fire," said Sickening Susan.

"Playing hide-and-seek in Whispering Woods," said Disgusting Denzil.

Basil sighed sadly. "It sounds like fun."

"Right, that settles it!" Denzil grabbed Basil's arm and waved it in the air. "Sir, Sir! Basil wants to come, too."

"Good," said Dr Grim. "I'll give you all a letter to take home to your parents."

Basil tried to look as pleased as everyone else about the Summer Camp. But underneath, he was very, very worried.

What if the other kids found out his shameful secret? They might laugh at him. Worse, they might not want to be friends with him any more. They might never speak to him again.

And all because ...

(This is Basil's shameful secret. Look away if you don't want to be shocked.)

Once a month, when the moon was full, he turned into a BOY!

Chapter 2

Summer Camp

Basil's mother read the letter from
Dr Grim.

"Summer Camp? That sounds like
fun," she said, and passed it to his
father.

"I used to enjoy camping when I
was a kid," said Dad. "Course you can
go, son."

"But I *can't!*" wailed Basil. "I've
worked it out. On July the 29th there'll
be a full moon."

"Oh, I see," said Mum. "You're afraid the others will find out?"

Basil nodded. He was nearly in tears. "Why does this have to happen to me?" he asked.

"Because Mad Mabel put a spell on you, that's why," said Dad. "We should never have asked her to be your godmother. She always did have a strange sense of humour."

"We'd ask her to undo the magic,"
said Mum. "But we
don't know where
she is."

Dad put his arm round Basil's
shoulders. "Listen, son. You mustn't let
this stop you going to camp. Why
should the others find out? After all,
the spell only lasts from midnight until
dawn. Everyone will be asleep."

"Your father's right," said Mum. "Go and enjoy yourself, Basil. Just take care, that's all."

Basil was torn in two. Half of him was scared about what might happen.

The other half badly wanted to have fun at Summer Camp with his friends.

"All right," he said at last. "I'll go."

* * *

"Great!" said Disgusting Denzil when Basil told him the news. "Let's ask if we can share a tent. You won't mind me snoring, will you?"

"Not a bit," said Basil.

To his surprise he found he was beginning to look forward to the Summer Camp. As time went on, he grew more and more excited. Mum even bought him a brand new backpack.

At last the great day arrived! Fifty
little monsters, together with Dr Grim
and Miss Peabody, climbed on to
the coach. They set off for
Whispering Woods.

"I wonder if we'll see Spooky Sybil,"
said Sickening Susan. (Spooky Sybil
was a wise old monster who lived in
Whispering Woods.) "People say she's
really, really weird!"

"I don't care if we do," said Boastful
Bertha. "She doesn't scare *me*!"

As soon as they reached the campsite they put up their tents.

That night, they had a delicious supper of squid soup and fried cowpats.

Then they had a singsong round the camp fire. They sang all their favourite monster songs, such as *Ten Green Vampires* and *Ging Gang Ghoulie*.

Basil was really, really glad he had come.

But as the week went on he began to feel more and more nervous. And when July 29th arrived, he felt too scared to go to bed.

"Lovely full moon," said Denzil, as he crawled into the tent that night.

"Yes, it is," Basil agreed unhappily.

He zipped up his sleeping bag and closed his eyes. But he knew he wouldn't sleep a single wink. He lay there, scared, waiting to change.

Chapter 3

A Horrible Sight

Disgusting Denzil stirred in his sleep.
Something had woken him – a furtive,
rustling noise.

Cautiously, he lifted his head. In the
dim light he could just see Basil's
shadowy figure leaving the tent.

Was he sleepwalking?

Denzil caught his breath.
Sleepwalking was dangerous. Basil
might fall into a hole ... or bump into
a tree. He must go after him.

Denzil crawled out of the tent and
looked around. Luckily the moon was
bright so he could see quite clearly.

But where was Basil?
Ah, there he was.

Denzil followed Basil into the wood.
The leaves shivered in the breeze.
They filled the night with their strange
rustling voices. "Watch out, Denzil,"
they warned. "Take care ..."

Now he knew why they were called
the Whispering Woods!

Suddenly Basil groaned and fell to
his knees. Denzil rushed forward to
help him up, but he got the most
terrible shock.

Gone was Basil's long, shaggy hair. Instead his hair was short and fair and very neat.

Gone were Basil's pointed yellow teeth. Instead his teeth were white and even.

Gone were Basil's gleaming dark eyes. Instead his eyes were bright blue.

Gone was his purple-spotted skin. Instead his skin was pale and smooth.

He looked *horrible*!

Denzil covered his eyes. He had seen pictures of ugly creatures like this. They were called 'boys'.

But he had thought they only existed in books. He had never expected to meet one in real life.

"Oh, Den!" cried Basil. "You shouldn't have followed me. I knew you'd be shocked. But I can't help it. It happens every time there's a full moon."

"W-w-why?" Denzil stammered.

"A woman called Mad Mabel put a spell on me when I was a baby," said Basil. "It doesn't last long – only from midnight until dawn. But we can't ask her to undo it. We don't know where she is."

Denzil felt sick with horror. But he
saw the misery and pain in Basil's
strange blue eyes and he felt sorry
for him.

"Why don't you ask Spooky Sybil
to change the spell?" he asked. "She
knows a lot about magic."

"What – now?" asked Basil, nervously.

"Best to go while the spell's still on you," said Denzil. "Then she can see what the problem is."

Basil hesitated. "I'll go if you'll come with me," he said at last. "I'm too scared to go on my own."

"Oh, all right," said Denzil, shakily.

Chapter 4

Spooky Sybil

Spooky Sybil's hut was hidden deep among the trees. Smoke curled from a chimney even though it was summertime. A green light shone in the window.

"Go on, Baz," said Disgusting Denzil. "Knock on the door."

Basil hesitated. "She might not be friendly. People say she is really weird. She might even put a worse spell on me."

"It's worth a try," said Denzil. "You don't want to be stuck with this problem for the rest of your life."

"No, I don't," agreed Basil. Nervously, he knocked on the door.

It opened almost at once. Spooky
Sybil stood in the doorway.

Her wild green hair was sticking up
all over her head. An owl sat on one
shoulder; a mouse on the other.

"Yes?" she said in an unfriendly voice.

Denzil said boldly, "My friend Basil needs your help. You see, every time there's a full moon, *this* happens to him." He pulled Basil forward into the light.

"Sssssss!" Spooky Sybil was clearly shocked. "This looks like Mad Mabel's work. Am I right?"

Basil nodded, miserably. "Please –
can you undo the spell?"

"Come inside." Spooky Sybil stood
back to let them come in.

A strange green glow filled the hut.
Small woodland creatures scurried
across the floor. They climbed up the
table legs to munch on bread and
pieces of cheese.

Spiders hung from the ceiling. A fox
lay curled up on the bed.

Spooky Sybil glared at them both.
"I don't see why I should help you.
You young monsters make far too
much noise and scare my animals."

"We don't do it on purpose," said
Basil. He stroked the fox's head.

Spooky Sybil watched him. At last
she said, "Oh all right then. Hold this."

She handed Basil a small mirror. "Don't look into it until I tell you to."

Nervously Basil gripped the mirror.

Spooky Sybil took several bottles off the shelf. She poured the contents into a jug.

Next, she added some powder from a jar and some dried leaves. Then she held the jug under the owl's beak and said, "Sneeze!"

The owl sneezed into the potion.

Spooky Sybil stirred the greenish-greyish liquid. She poured out a glass and handed it to Basil. "Drink it up – every drop," she ordered.

Basil screwed up his eyes and drank. Denzil held his breath.

At first nothing seemed to happen.

Then slowly, Basil started to turn bright green.

He grew brighter and brighter until finally he disappeared inside a huge green bubble.

Denzil watched fearfully. Would he ever see his friend again?

The bubble burst. And there stood
Basil, just as handsome as he was
before. Denzil breathed a huge sigh of
relief.

"Now you can look in the mirror,"
said Spooky Sybil.

Basil looked in the mirror. He gasped with delight. "Oh how can I ever thank you?" he asked Spooky Sybil.

"Just be kind to all animals, birds and insects," she told him. "That's the only reward I ask. And remember – keep away from mad old women called Mabel."

"I will," promised Basil.

They returned to the camp to find the lights blazing. Everyone was running round in circles. The little monsters raced up to Basil and Denzil.

"Miss Peabody saw you were missing and raised the alarm," said Boastful Bertha.

"We thought you'd been kidnapped!"
said Sickening Susan.

Basil and Denzil grinned at each
other. "No, we weren't kidnapped,"
said Basil. "It was such a beautiful
night we – er, went for a walk."

"You're so *brave!*" sighed Susan.
And all the other little monsters gazed
at them with admiration.

"Basil! Denzil!" Dr Grim and Miss
Peabody came rushing up to them.
"Where have you been?"

"They went for a walk," said
Boastful Bertha.

"A walk – in the middle of the
night?" Miss Peabody looked shocked.
"We've been worried sick about you."

"Sorry," muttered Basil and Denzil
together.

"All right everyone, back to your
tents," called Dr Grim. "I think we've
had enough excitement for one night."

Basil agreed. He'd had more than enough excitement. But now, thanks to Spooky Sybil, he need no longer be afraid of the full moon.

The spell was undone. Never again would he be changed into that scary creature called a 'boy'.

He couldn't *wait* to tell Mum and Dad!

About the author

I wrote my first story when I was four years old. From that moment I knew I wanted to be a writer, but it was many years before my first book (which was about dinosaurs) was published. Since then I've written many stories, mostly about animals.

Disgusting Denzil was my first ever story about a little monster. I enjoyed writing it so much that I decided to write another, this time about Denzil's friend, Beastly Basil.